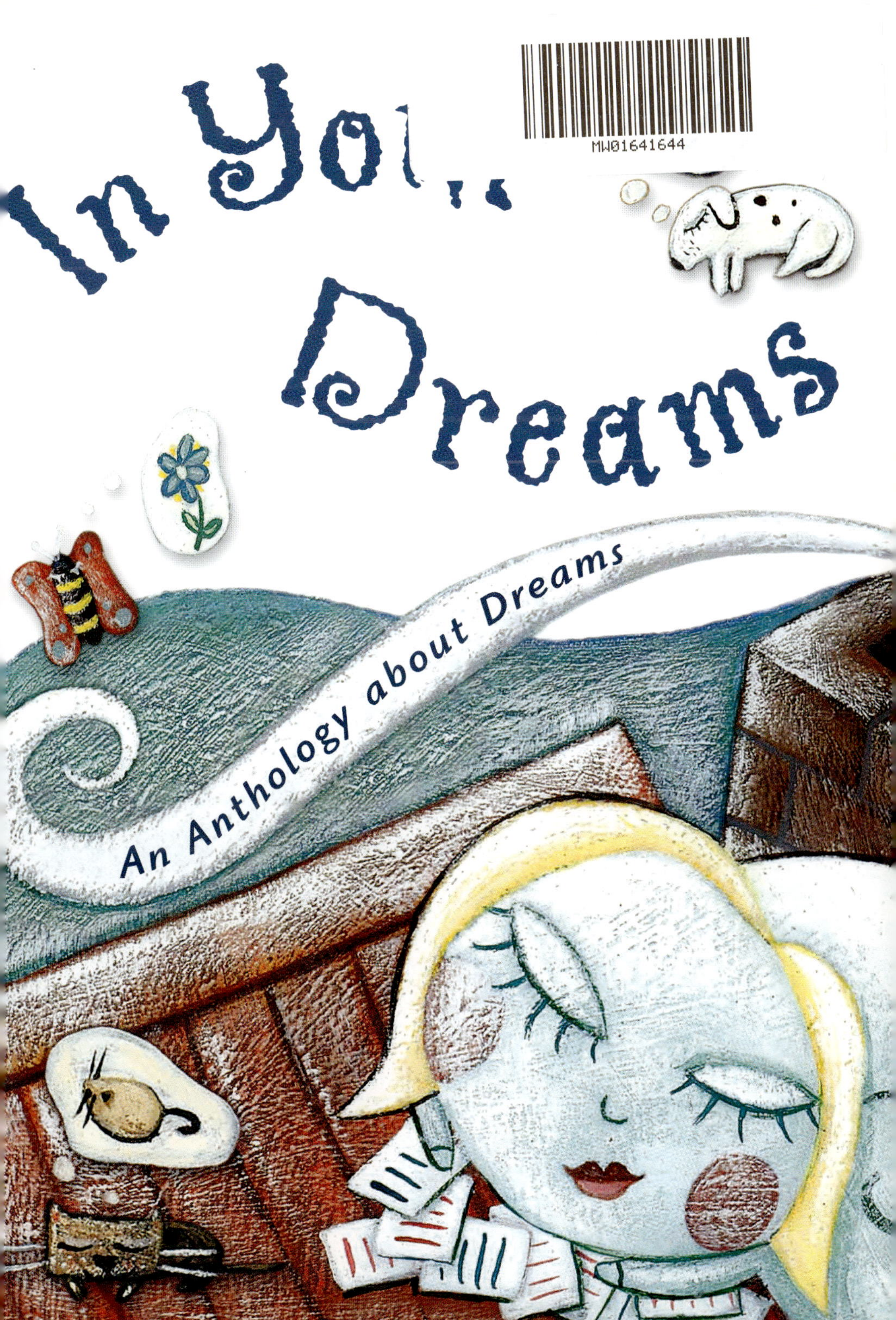
In Yo…
Dreams
An Anthology about Dreams
MW01641644

PM Anthology
part of the Rigby PM Collection

U.S. edition © 2001 Rigby
A division of Reed Elsevier Inc.
1000 Hart Road
Barrington, IL 60010–2627
www.rigby.com

06 05 04 03 02 01
10 9 8 7 6 5 4 3 2 1

In Your Dreams: An Anthology about Dreams
ISBN 0 7578 1171 X

Designed by Catherine Squared Pty Ltd
Photographs on Contents, pp.30, 33 by Bill Thomas
Cover illustration by Amanda Dawson

Acknowledgements:
The publisher would like to acknowledge the following authors and publishers for their permission to reprint excerpts from the titles below for this anthology:

'The Dream' by Itane Sekyrková from *Modern Tales and Fables*, Paul Hamlyn, 1967; 'Hold Fast to Dreams' by Langston Hughes from *The Collected Poems of Langston Hughes*, Alfred A. Knopf Inc, USA, 1994; *The Dream Snatcher* by Kara May, Collins, Harper Collins Publishers, London, England, 1988; 'The Peddler of Swaffham' from *Folktales and Fables of Europe*, Chelsea House Publishers, 1992; 'Live Your Dreams' extract from *Lionheart: A Journey of the Human Spirit* by Jesse Martin, Allen & Unwin, Sydney, Australia, 2000; 'Safe in the Harbor' by Eric Bogle, © Larrikin Music Publishing Pty Ltd; *The Lifesaver* by Nicole Plüss, Kindrid, Curtis Brown, Sydney, Australia, 1995; 'Dream of Krakatao' by Carroll B. Colby from *Strangely Enough*, Sterling Publishing Company, NY, USA, 1959.

Printed in China by Midas Printing (Asia) Ltd

Contents

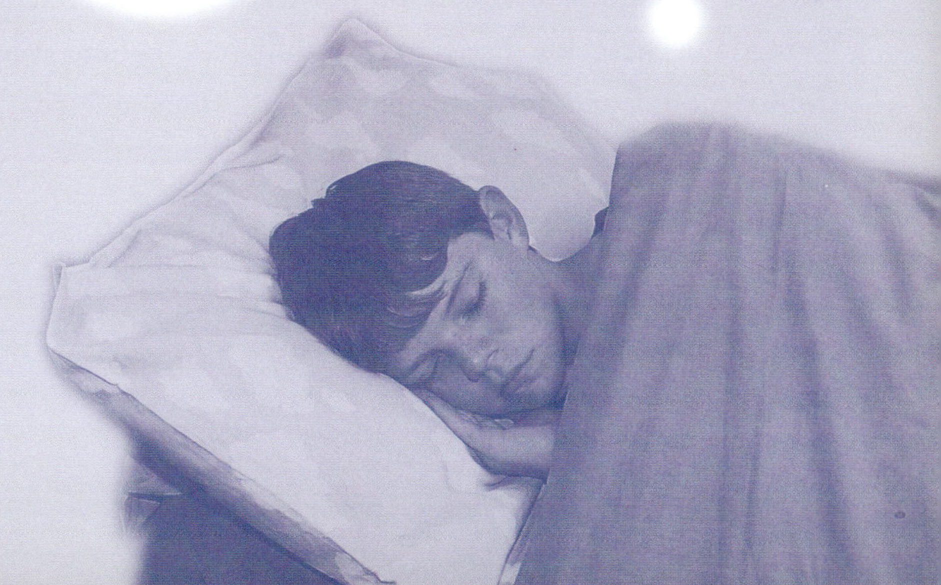

The Dream

Itane Sekyrková Illustrated by Amanda Dawson

There was a dream which did not want to be dreamed. It made a nest for itself out of lullabies behind the chimney on a red roof, made itself all snug and cozy, and fell asleep.

A sparrow mother flew past and she tried to wake the dream.

"Come, come, come with me. Come and be dreamed by my baby bird."

The dream opened just one eye, stared at the sparrow mother, and retorted: "I'm no sparrow-dream about earthworms, you know. You've come to the wrong address." And the dream turned over on its other side and fell asleep once more.

Nor did the little dog manage to make it come along and be dreamed, nor the horse, nor the paper kite, the flower from the window box, or Cleopatra the black cat from the alley apartment.

The dream slept on — and it slept until the late afternoon. The sun had just given a yawn, covered itself with a cloud, and decided to turn in for the night. The dream would most probably not have woken even then, had it not been tickled under the nose by the chimney sweep's brush. Jack Dodge, the chimney sweep, had just finished work for the day and was about to go home to his supper when he saw someone sleeping behind the chimney.

"Well, well, isn't this a nice surprise," said Jack Dodge, the chimney sweep, when he saw who it was. "A dream. I'll take you home to my three boys. They're always pestering me to bring something home for them."

"What? Am I to be dreamed by a lot of dirty chimney sweeps?" said the dream proudly. "Not on your life! I wasn't born for *that*. I'm the nicest dream that ever was."

"Are you really?" asked the chimney sweep. "And what are you *about*?"

"I am … why, I am … a beautiful dream … the most beautiful dream of all … about … about …" The dream stammered, unable to remember what it was really about. It had slept so long that it could not remember anything.

"If that's what you're like, my boys wouldn't want to have you," said the chimney sweep, laughing. "A dream — and it doesn't know what it is all about!" Jack Dodge turned his back on the dream, picked up his brush, and before you could say Jack Robinson, he was down in the street, and before you could have repeated it two more times, had vanished around the corner.

The dream was left behind feeling very sorry for itself. It was almost dark by now and before long it should have started being dreamed by somebody. It was on the point of bursting into tears, but then it thought better of it — it wouldn't do to make the roof all slippery with tears.

So the dream just sniveled a little as it walked slowly along the gutter and down into the street, then into another and yet another street, looking in all the windows (dreams may do that without being rude).

Everywhere it saw children asleep — chimney sweeps' children and bakers' and gardeners' and carpenters' children and all the other children as well — and cats and dogs asleep, the flowers in their gardens, and the toys on their shelves. All of them had been rocked to sleep by some dream or other — all of them were dreaming nicely.

The dream this story is about stood underneath a lamppost, very annoyed with itself for having been such a stuck-up, nasty little beast. If only it could find at least one single creature who had no dream of his own and would start dreaming it.

All of a sudden it heard a cheeping noise from up above. “Cheep” and then three more times, “cheep, cheep, cheep.” And there, just under the lamp, was an untidy nest and leaning out of it was a tiny sparrow. All alone. Its mother was probably still trying to find a dream for it. Anyone know of one? Why, of course — there it came, climbing and clambering up the lamppost and, hop, it was inside the nest. The dream from our fairy tale. It made the little bird nice and comfy in one corner of the nest, took it in its arms, and rocked it, humming a little tune. And as soon as the tiny sparrow had closed its eyes, the dream knew what it was to be about: about an earthworm and the sun, about raindrops threaded on a string, and about a lovely big slice of bread.

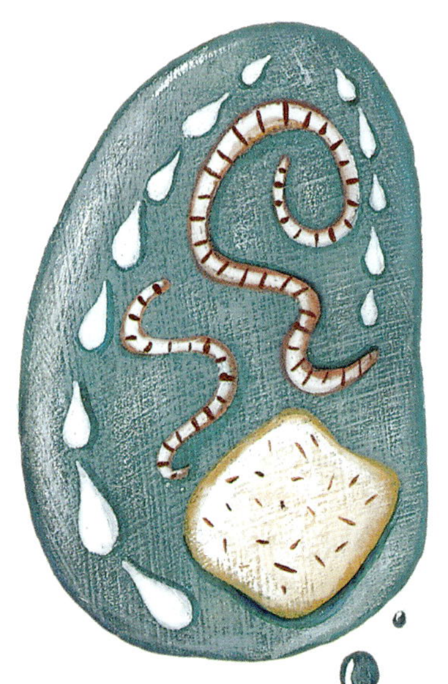

When it woke next morning, the little bird said to its mother: "I had the loveliest dream last night."

The dream heard this, as it was on its way back to the chimney on the red rooftop, and it thought how nice it was to be a dream. An ordinary, nice dream — and what did it matter if it was dreamed by a mere little sparrow. ◆

Hold Fast to Dreams

Langston Hughes   Illustrated by Dominique Falla

Hold fast to dreams
For if dreams die
Life is a broken-winged bird
That cannot fly.
Hold fast to dreams
For when dreams go
Life is a barren field
Frozen with snow.

The Dream Snatcher

Kara May Illustrated by Kevin Burgemeestre

The mysterious Dream Snatcher offers to pay a cup of gold to all who sell him their dreams. There is no harm in that, the townspeople think. But Jodie doesn't agree. Never sell your dreams, Grandma once told her.

Jodie decides to heed Grandma's words, but watches in despair as her uncle, cousins, and the rest of the town sell their dreams. Soon, the townspeople can't dream enough dreams for the powerful Dream Snatcher, and he threatens to destroy their town.

Setting the Scene

The Dream Snatcher has just arrived in town, and has bought everyone's dreams. Jodie remembers Grandma's warning, and decides not to sell her dreams. She turns to go, but is quickly noticed by the Dream Snatcher. He orders her to stop, and then marches menacingly toward her …

Jodie stood with her fists gripped by her sides and lowered her eyes as the Stranger came toward her.

"What's your name, girl?" he rasped.

"My name is Jodie," she whispered.

She was aware that everyone was staring at her. Not just the Stranger, but the people, too. A sudden hush fell. She was desperate for something to fill it.

"Please, what's *your* name?" she blurted.

The Stranger started. "My name!" he growled. "You ask my name, girl!"

"She'll be in for it now! She's made him angry," muttered the people.

Jodie gripped her fists more tightly and waited for the blasting to come. But when at last the Stranger spoke, his voice wasn't angry. It sounded flat and dull as if the feeling were all drained out.

"You can call me the Dream Snatcher," he said with a shrug. "Why not? It's what I do. But enough of all this! To business, girl," the Dream Snatcher rapped out abruptly. "A cup of gold for your dreams. Is it a deal? Yes or no?"

He took it she'd answer "yes" and he held out the cup of gold. Jodie didn't dare refuse and she reached out her hand to take it. Like a flame of fire, her grandma's warning burst into her mind: Never sell your dreams.

She'd always meant to ask her grandma, why not? It was too late for that now. But one thing was certain, thought Jodie. Her grandma had never let her down or harmed her — not once, not ever.

She took a deep breath.

"My dreams are not for sale," she said.

The people gasped.

"Hmph! Please yourself, girl," said the Dream Snatcher.

That was it!

He waved her off.

Jodie couldn't believe it. She took her chance and fled.

She ran home and went to her room till she saw her family come down the street. They were clutching their cups of gold. She'd never seen her uncle look so happy, but when he saw her, he greeted her with a stony stare.

"So, here's the little miss who had her chance to be rich and turned up her nose at it."

"But ..." began Jodie. She wanted to tell him what her grandma had told her. Her uncle cut her short.

"Don't ask me for a handout. You won't get it, Miss!"

"Don't go asking us, either!" chimed in her cousins. "You're not getting your mitts on our money."

"I wasn't going to ask," answered Jodie, and went back to her room.

That night when the moon was up, Jodie stirred in her sleep and suddenly woke. She got up and went to the window.

"The Dream Snatcher! Here he comes!"

She watched as he came down the street. He held the Dream Box over his head, turning it this way and that. She saw it flash with colors as it snatched up the dreams from the people as they slept.

"What will he do with them?" she wondered. She was still wondering as she went back to bed.

In a dream of her own, she saw the Dream Snatcher make his way through the shopping center up to the parking lot. A screen ran the full length of one wall. There was an assortment of gadgets underneath it. He slotted the Dream Box into one of them. At once a red rabbit appeared on the screen. It was standing on its head, eating a banana, and wearing a skirt made of cabbage leaves! Whose dream was it? Jodie smiled in her sleep. Alf the Butcher's perhaps!

She saw one dream after another flash onto the screen. Sad dreams, weird dreams, funny dreams, cruel dreams. The Dream Snatcher watched them all, stretched out on the cold, concrete floor. At last the screen went blank. He hauled himself to his feet and began to stamp around.

That was the last thing Jodie remembered when she woke up the next morning. She was sure that what she'd seen had truly happened. But she had a question that she asked her uncle.

"Why does the Dream Snatcher buy other people's dreams?" she asked. "Why doesn't he dream his own?"

"Who cares!" snorted her uncle. "What he does is up to him. We've got our money and we're going to spend it."

"Spend! Spend! Spend!" shrieked her cousins.

Her uncle clapped his hands. "To the shopping center! Let's go!"

Jodie watched as they went running gleefully down the street. All over the town it was the same. People went on a spend! spend! spend! bonanza. They installed the newest appliances in their homes, bought flashy cars, designer clothes, clever gadgets — whatever they fancied. The children filled their shelves with toys and computers and mountain bikes and paraded around in all of the latest gear.

All except Jodie.

She was still wearing her cousins' hand-me-downs.

The other children had often picked on her, even when her grandma was alive. There was no stopping them now.

"A scarecrow looks smarter than you!" they jeered. "You haven't even got your own TV or computer. You're a nobody, Jodie!"

"Jodie Nobody! Jodie Nobody!"

They danced around her and chanted it, over and over. Her cousins joined in.

"You've no one to blame but yourself," said her uncle. "You could have been as rich as the rest of us. But no, you'd sooner have your dreams — which are no use to man or beast!"

Jodie went again to explain about her grandma's warning, but no one was listening.

Her cousins sniggered, "Jodie Nobody."

It became a nickname that everyone called her.

Her uncle treated her as if he still was poor. She had mostly bread and butter to eat with not even jam for a treat. He fixed up the house and even built a patio and addition but he left her room as it was, with a bare wooden floor and a crack in the window where the wind howled in.

"You can dream yourself warm, Jodie Nobody," smirked her cousins. "We're going shopping."

The shopping center stayed open all night, as well as the restaurants. People went from one to the other. There was no point in going to bed — they never really slept. Since they'd sold their dreams it was as if a part of them was missing, and they tossed and turned all night, trying to find them. But they weren't too bothered.

"If we can't sleep, we'll shop and have fun instead. After all, we can afford it."

Her cousins told Jodie they were having a party.

"We've got a new sound system," they crowed. "It'll be the best party ever!"

"I'll help you get things ready. Please may I come?" she asked.

They looked at her as if she were something yucky that had crawled out from under a stone.

"You've got to be joking! We don't want you at our party, Jodie Nobody. Keep out or else!"

They locked her in her room when the party started. Jodie sat on her bed, too miserable even to turn on the light. To cheer herself up, she went over last night's funny dream where she wasn't herself, but an ostrich! She'd buried her head not in the sand, but in a freezer. Then the ice melted and —

Suddenly she heard footsteps out in the street.

"The Dream Snatcher! I knew he'd come! He hasn't missed a night yet."

Jodie ran to the window. The Dream Snatcher was shaking the Dream Box as if it were a clock he was trying to make tick. It flashed slowly once or twice. Jodie wasn't surprised! With the music from the party throbbing over the rooftops, it'd be hard for people to sleep, much less dream.

The Dream Snatcher thrust the Dream Box into his pocket.

And looked up.

And saw her.

She was always careful to hide behind the curtain when she watched him go by. But with the party going on, she'd forgotten.

What should she do?

Was it up to her to say "hello!" or something?

The words froze in her throat.

She just stared.

The Dream Snatcher stared back.

At last he strode off.

"Whew!" breathed Jodie.

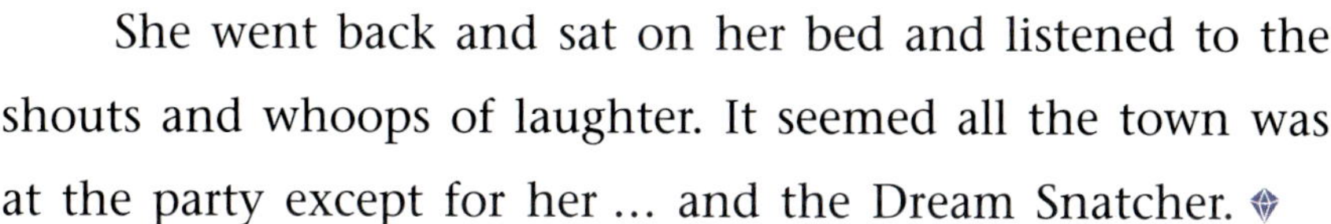

She went back and sat on her bed and listened to the shouts and whoops of laughter. It seemed all the town was at the party except for her ... and the Dream Snatcher.

Eventually, the townspeople run out of dreams for the Dream Snatcher. Only Jodie has dreams left. The Dream Snatcher threatens to blow up the town unless she sells him her dreams. So Jodie faces the Dream Snatcher, alone. But she doesn't sell her dreams; instead, she teaches the Dream Snatcher how to dream.

In Your Dreams

Dreams by Year 6 students

Illustrated by Melissa Webb

In the greatest dream
I've ever had, I lived in a
chocolate land and everything
was chocolate!

EMMA

The greatest dream
I've ever had was when I was
riding a white pony.
I was riding toward
my hopes.

SIAN

*I am happy about most
of my life, but I have a dream
to change all the bad things
in life to good things.*

ELLIOT

My greatest dream was flying
in the air, hundreds of feet above
the ground, and never stopping.

PRUE

The greatest dream
I have is that everyone's
dreams come true.
It would make a perfect world!

EMILY

In my ideal world, a dreamworld
of fantasy and medieval times,
I would be a warrior or a
famous archer.

EVAN

Control Your Dreams

Louise Schofield Illustrated by Rob Mancini
Photographs by Bill Thomas

The people of the Senoi tribe of Malaysia were considered the happiest people in the world. Well, that's what some psychologists believed following studies of the tribe released in the 1970s.

Psychologists help people cope with and overcome problems that are making their lives unhappy. Some psychologists believed that the Senoi tribe's approach to dreaming helped its people live happy, peaceful lives.

The Senoi people lived in the mountain jungles of Malaysia. Their tribal life was quite different from the fast-paced, materialistic lifestyle that most of us experience. The Senoi tribe fascinated psychologists because its people had little or no experience with the violence, fears, and mental illnesses that often occur in our society.

The Senoi people lived in a peaceful and cooperative community. Other tribes living similar lifestyles in the jungles around them still experienced wars and anxieties. So what was the Senoi's secret?

Their secret was their dreams.

The Senoi people had learned to control their dreams, and in turn, learn from these nighttime experiences. Every morning the people shared their dreams with the community. Children were instructed on how to make their dreams happier and how to defeat their dream enemies – the causes of their nightmares.

By the time Senoi children were teenagers, they had no more nightmares. Community projects were also enriched by the creative ideas that had been found in their dreams.

You can also learn to control your dreams like the Senoi people. With practice, you will make your dreams happier. As a result, your daytime life is likely to be happier as well.

Dream Guidelines

When you wake up from a dream, try to *remember* the dream before you forget it. With practice, remembering will become easier.

If your dream was unpleasant, or if it was a nightmare, *think how you might have changed it* into a happy experience. Even if the dream had been just OK, imagine how you could have made it more enjoyable. Always look for happiness.

Teach yourself to become aware of your dreams *as they are happening*. Don't wake up! Learn to *participate* in your dreams, rather than just letting them happen. Take control and enjoy them.

If you are being attacked in a nightmare, face your attacker and will it to go away. *Confront and conquer danger* in your dreams. This is an important rule in the Senoi system.

If you are falling in a dream, *land safely in a wonderful place*. Next time, try to fly instead.

If you defeat an enemy, ask it for a *gift* — preferably something that you can use in your waking life — a song, a poem, a story, or an idea for a project. If you have landed in a special place, go in search of such a gift.

Do not leave a dream without a happy ending.

Remember: anything bad in your dreamworld can't really hurt you. That dream tiger or monster won't harm you if you face it. You have so much to gain in confidence and happiness if you defeat your fears and control your dreams.

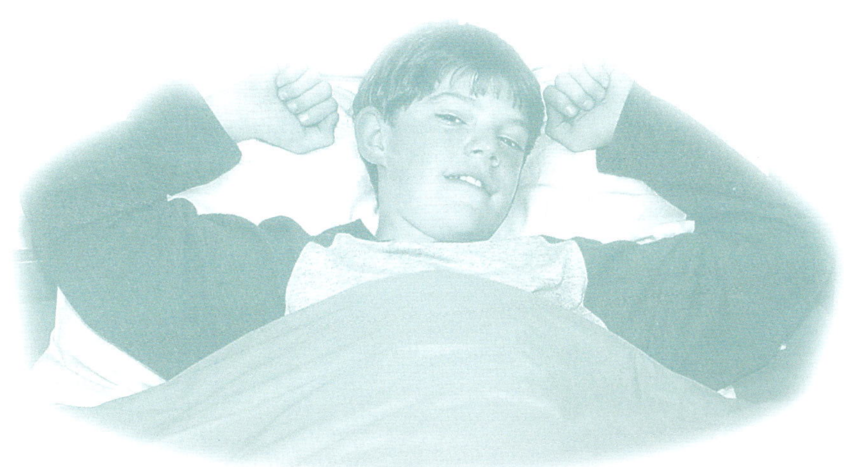

The Peddler of Swaffham

Illustrated by Debbie Mourtzios

This story dates from the Middle Ages, when London Bridge was lined on both sides with shops and houses. The legendary peddler is commemorated in Swaffham's town sign and there is a carved statue of him inside a building.

Legend has it that hundreds of years ago, in the village of Swaffham, in the county of Norfolk in England, there lived a peddler who was constantly having the same dream. A voice told the peddler that if he went and stood on London Bridge, he would hear joyful news.

At first the peddler paid no attention. A journey to London would not be easy. It was nearly one hundred miles to London, so it would take him two or three days to walk there. And he would have to sleep in barns or hedges along the way.

But the dream persisted, and the voice was so insistent that the peddler became upset and worried. He began to dread going upstairs to bed.

At last he said to his wife, "It is no use. I shall have to go to London and stand on London Bridge or I shall have no peace for the rest of my life."

He packed a few belongings, some food, and a little money. He whistled to his dog, and they walked the long road to London.

In those days, London Bridge was a bustling place with houses and shops on either side of the roadway. It was the only way across the Thames River unless you went by boat. For several days the peddler stood on the bridge, first in one spot and then another, but no one spoke to him and no one gave him joyful news.

I was a fool to come, he told himself, but still he waited.

Finally, when he had nothing but a crust of bread in his pocket and knew that he must leave for Norfolk within the hour, a shopkeeper stepped out of his shop and came and spoke to him.

"Satisfy my curiosity," said the shopkeeper. "I have seen you here for several days. You do not beg, you do not pick pockets, you are not selling anything. Why are you standing here?"

The peddler replied honestly that he had dreamed that if he stood on London Bridge, he would hear joyful news.

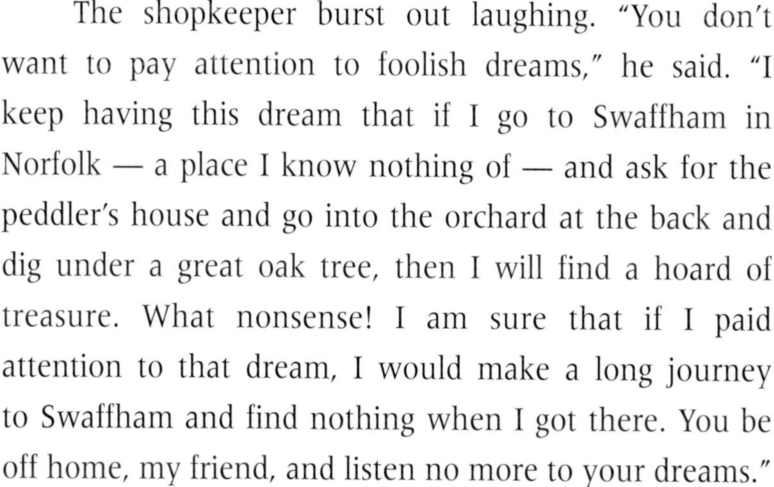

The shopkeeper burst out laughing. "You don't want to pay attention to foolish dreams," he said. "I keep having this dream that if I go to Swaffham in Norfolk — a place I know nothing of — and ask for the peddler's house and go into the orchard at the back and dig under a great oak tree, then I will find a hoard of treasure. What nonsense! I am sure that if I paid attention to that dream, I would make a long journey to Swaffham and find nothing when I got there. You be off home, my friend, and listen no more to your dreams."

The peddler hurried home to Swaffham. He went into the orchard at the back of his house and dug under the great oak tree. He found a treasure chest and was wealthy for the rest of his life. ◆

Live Your Dreams

Jesse Martin

Eighteen-year-old Jesse Martin left Melbourne, Australia, on December 7, 1998, and sailed 30,000 miles around the world.

He arrived back in Melbourne on October 31, 1999. He became the youngest person to sail nonstop, solo, and unassisted around the world.

The world is a funny place.

It's hard to imagine, as you stand in your backyard or lie in your bed, that there is a spot on this amazing globe directly opposite you. If you drilled a hole directly through the earth, where would you come out?

At 5:36 PM on December 7, 1998, I sailed from the safety of my home waters of Melbourne, Australia, on my 34-foot yacht Lionheart, and set course for that other point — latitude 38°18'N longitude 35°22'W. And when I got there, I kept going, returning to Melbourne on October 31, 1999, 328 days and roughly 27,000 nautical miles later. In my quest, I became the youngest person to circumnavigate the globe solo, nonstop, and unassisted.

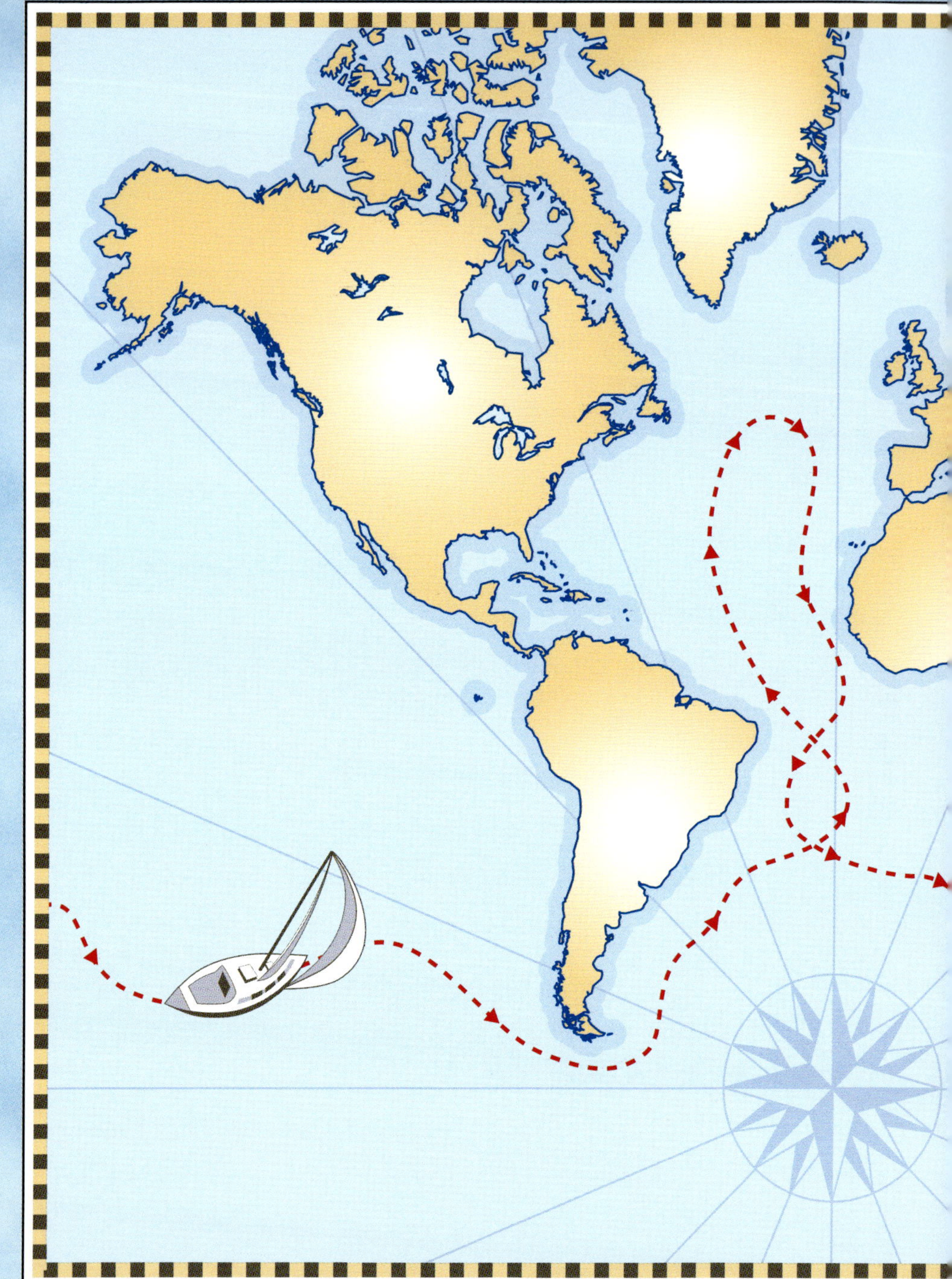

I had dreamt of sailing around the world, so that's what I did.

If we don't live our dreams, what's the point of living?

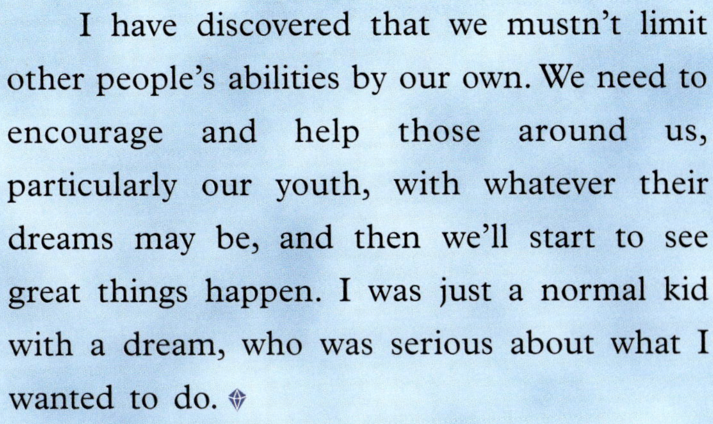

I have discovered that we mustn't limit other people's abilities by our own. We need to encourage and help those around us, particularly our youth, with whatever their dreams may be, and then we'll start to see great things happen. I was just a normal kid with a dream, who was serious about what I wanted to do. ♦

Safe in the Harbor

Eric Bogle

So when storm clouds come sailing across your blue ocean,
Hold fast to your dreaming for all that you're worth
For as long as there's dreamers, there will always be sailors
Bringing back their bright treasures from the corners of the earth.

But to every sailor comes time to drop anchor
Haul in the sails, and make lines fast
You deep water dreamer, your journey is over
You're safe in the harbor at last
You're safe in the harbor at last.

The Lifesaver

Nicole Plüss Illustrated by Bettina Guthridge

Jeremy is spending his summer at the beach with Dad and Trina, Dad's girlfriend. One day, he sees a girl somersaulting through the waves. Then she disappears under the waves and never resurfaces. Jeremy's sure that she has drowned. Sandie, the lifeguard, refuses to believe him. There was no girl in the waves, she says. But Jeremy knows Sandie is hiding something …

A mysterious old woman gives him a clue — the girl's name is Maire. Finally, Sandie reveals a chilling tale about a girl called Maire who drowned over a hundred years ago.

But there's still something else mysterious about Maire — Jeremy can feel it. Something powerful, something magical …

Setting the Scene

Jeremy is in real trouble. He was caught in Maire's Rip, and is dragged out to open sea. The ocean swell is growing and Jeremy is helpless, struggling to stay afloat in the huge waves. There's also something large swimming beneath him, something gray and dangerous. And looming ahead are sharp coastal rocks...

I felt the flash of movement again, this time to my side. I knew it would be better not to look, but I couldn't help myself. I don't understand how it is possible to be so scared and still be alive. If I had stretched my hand across, I could have touched it. Smooth and silent. An endless, gray expanse. I'd never realized that sharks were so big — much bigger than me. I hoped I'd die of heart failure. I'd rather anything than be attacked by a shark. Even being smashed into a million pieces against the rocks. The shark disappeared from sight on one side and then loomed into view on the other. Its head came level with mine. One eye slowly passed, unblinking as it studied me. I looked right into the eye of the shark. I felt like my heart was going to stop.

Yet even in my panic, I could see that there was something strange about this shark. There was something very odd in the way it was looking at me. Perhaps it didn't know what I was. It circled again and glided up the other side. Once again it looked at me. It regarded me with what seemed to be interest. Intelligent interest. I could almost see expression in its eye. Human expression. Then just as it was about to pass out of my line of sight, the eye winked very slowly. Do fish eyes wink? Do they have eyelids?

The ocean had rapidly changed under me. The water was starting to form the waves that smashed into the rocks. The swell was much higher, lifting and dropping me like a cork. I could no longer float on my back. I needed to swim to stay upright in the wild water. I couldn't see the shark anymore and I didn't have time to worry about it, anyway. The waves were roaring in my ears, continuously dunking me. They were so high, I was constantly struggling to the surface. I scanned the rock face, looking for a ledge I might be able to scramble onto, but all I could see was a steep, smooth expanse of rock. The lifeguards wouldn't be able to reach me now. Nothing could save me.

There was a short lull in the waves. I looked behind me and saw the reason for the calm. An enormous wave was gathering momentum. The second I looked at it I knew that I wouldn't survive it. If I stayed on the surface it would pick me up and carry me onward. I reacted without thinking and did exactly what I would do in the surf. I took a huge gulp of air and dived under it. I struggled to swim under the worst of the wave, but I was worried that if I swam too low then I might be lucky to even surface again. I thrashed my arms and legs to fight against the pull toward the rocks. I was tired.

My chest started hurting. I needed air, but I couldn't surface yet. I was still too close to the rocks. I couldn't seem to get away no matter how hard I tried. It was only then that I realized I might die, out there on my own, struggling hopelessly against something much stronger than me. I had always imagined death as something that approached slowly at the end of a long life, not something that swoops when you're still at school. The faces of Mom and Dad came into my mind, and I realized that I might never see them again.

Strange memories flashed into my mind. Smudge, my dog, who was run over when I was eight, and the way Dad had looked when I told him Mom was getting remarried.

No! I thought violently. No! I don't want to die. I haven't even started living yet! I haven't had a chance to live! I thrashed in the water in a last, desperate flurry to surface, but I was very deep now and the water was rough and wild. I wasn't going to make it.

Suddenly the water beneath me was colder and I felt a solid object rising beneath my legs. I couldn't see exactly what it was. I put my hands down to feel it. It was cold and smooth. It moved beneath my hands and lifted under me so I was lying along its length. I no longer had to support myself in the water. Suddenly I realized what it was. My feet pressed against its tail. My stomach lay along its smooth, gray back. Without thinking, I stretched forward and grabbed the fin as we started to move upward.

Its tail flicked once with great power and we surfaced in a matter of seconds well away from the rock face. In a burst I could see the rocks that had been so close and the endless expanse of water in front of us. I breathed in heavy gasps as I looked at the flat head of the shark in the water beneath me. At that moment I knew it wasn't a shark. I knew who it was. I knew … Don't drown me, I thought. Oh please, Maire. No matter what happened to you all those years ago, please don't drown me.

With another flick of her tail, we crashed through the waves. The water rushed past us furiously. We swam at a tremendous speed, yet I wasn't frightened. All I felt was pure exhilaration. It was the most amazing feeling. I pressed myself against her as hard as I could and tried to move with her. Twisting and turning in the sea. I felt a surging power I'd never imagined possible in the water. I felt like a creature of the sea. Streamlined and slim. The water rushed around my body.

As we burst through to the surface, the sun dazzled my eyes and the breeze was sharp in my face. When I looked down, I could see Maire beneath me. Her strong body moving with so little effort and yet so much power. Her beautiful silver-gray skin glinting in the sunlight. I felt like laughing out loud in sheer joy.

The water gradually changed around us. It was shallow and churning. I lifted my face from the waves and caught a glimpse of the shore. A flash of pine trees against the blue sky. A few splashes of color and running figures. The smell of land. I felt the swell of the breakers before I could hear the waves crashing onto the sand. She had taken me in. "Thank you, Maire," I thought. "Thank you." Her body lowered mine in the water. Her tail flashed beneath me. As the first wave dumped on my head, I let her go.

I was immediately surrounded by legs in the water and people reaching down and clutching me. One grip was by far stronger than the others. Dad dragged me out of the water and halfway up the beach. He was screaming and shouting. I could hardly hear him. I was smiling sweetly. I was floating. I was still in another world.

"Are you all right?" Dad shouted in my face.

I nodded, still dreamy.

"He's rolling his eyes!" Dad cried. "He's going to pass out."

He shook me. My mind tensed immediately.

"Jeremy, look at me and tell me you're all right."

I looked at Dad above me. His anxious eyes fixed desperately on my face.

"I'm all right," I whispered, and then surprised myself by bursting into tears.

"You floated in," Trina whispered. "You came from nowhere. The boat is out there looking for you, but here you are. You came out of the water like a fish. How did you do it? How did you swim like that?"

"Don't start your fishy hocus-pocus now Trina, for heaven's sake," Dad snapped.

He propped me into sitting position and wrapped a towel around my shoulders. I was shaking and shivering all over. I wanted to be back in the water. I wanted to be with Maire and feel like that again.

"What happened?" Trina insisted. "How did you do it? What happened to you?"

"It wasn't me ..." I started to explain but had to stop before a coughing fit overcame me.

"Who was it, then?" Trina whispered when I had stopped coughing. "Tell us what happened, Jeremy."

"It was her," I smiled dreamily, looking at all the anxious faces around me.

Dad and Trina. The parents holding their children close. The young surfers. The kids my age with sunscreen on their noses. Then on the outside of the circle I saw another face. The old woman. Her eyes were warning me to be quiet. Suddenly Sandie was beside me. She put her hand on my shoulder. She glanced at the old woman and then they both looked back down at me. At that moment I understood what they had been trying to tell me. Something shifted inside me and locked into place. We had to keep her safe.

"Jeremy?" Dad persisted. "What was it? What did you see?"

"Nothing, Dad."

"You were about to say something. What was it?"

"I think the tide must have brought me in. I was very lucky."

The old woman nodded with satisfaction and then picked up her bucket and headed off down the beach. Sandie smiled and left me with Dad and Trina. ◆

Dream of Krakatao

Carroll B. Colby Illustrated by Rob Mancini

One of the strangest of all "dream predictions" took place in 1883, when a gentleman by the name of Edward Samson was the news editor of the *Boston Globe*.

One August evening, Edward Samson fell asleep in his office at the paper and had a truly terrifying dream. He awoke about three in the morning and staggered to his feet, dripping with perspiration and terribly shaken by what he had seen in his dream.

He had witnessed a whole island, in some distant ocean, blown apart before his eyes. In spite of it having been only a dream, the details had been so clear and realistic that he began to write them down as he recalled them.

He recorded where it had happened, on the island of Pralape, near Java, and went on to describe how the natives had been caught between floods of red-hot lava and the boiling waters of the sea around the doomed island.

He wrote of rivers of mud 50 feet high, of ear-shattering explosions inside the mountains of the island, and finally, of a great explosion which destroyed the entire island, causing it to sink beneath the sea forever.

He finished his report with trembling hands, wrote "Important!" across it and left it on the desk when he went home. There it was found by the editor later that morning.

Thinking it was some story that had come in over the wire during the night, the editor ran it on the front page with banner headlines. It was picked up by papers across the country and was the most sensational news of August the 29th.

Then Samson was called for more details. When he admitted it had only been the report of a dream and not a story from the wires, the editor was furious. He would not only have to admit that the whole story was a hoax, but that all the other papers had been taken in as well.

The *Globe* printed a retraction explaining what had happened, and Samson was promptly fired. But almost at that moment, unusual things were being reported around the world.

High waves began running along the West Coast. Tidal waves ran wild over Malaysia and India. Australia reported vast explosions in the Indian Ocean, and the greatest waves ever recorded crashed against a thousand shores the world over — so great, in fact, that they circled the globe three times. Could there be a connection between Samson's dream and the strange, physical happenings? The retraction was forgotten, and Samson was back on the payroll writing this new story.

Then more reports began to come in. Krakatao, a volcanic island, had exploded and vanished with all its thousands of inhabitants in the greatest explosion of history. This occurred at the very same time Edward Samson had "seen" it in his dream. About the only difference was that he had called it Pralape — but that, too, is another mysterious part of this astounding story. For years later, it was found that Pralape had been the native name of Krakatao, but had not been used for more than 100 years!

How had Edward Samson seen, in such detail, this great catastrophe happening thousands of miles across the globe? And why had he called it by a long-forgotten name used only by natives a century earlier? ◈

Cloud Pictures

William Shakespeare Illustrated by Melissa Webb

Sometimes we see a cloud that's dragonish;
A vapor sometimes like a bear or lion,
A towered citadel, a pendant rock,
A forkèd mountain, or blue promontory,
With trees upon't, that nod unto the world,
And mock our eyes with air.